The Child's World of
SELF-CONTROL

Copyright © 1997 by The Child's World®, Inc.
All rights reserved. No part of this book may be reproduced or uti-
lized in any form or by any means without written permission from
the publisher.
Printed in the U.S.A.

Library of Congress Cataloging in Publication Data

Gambill, Henrietta.
Self-control / Henrietta Gambill.
p.   cm.
Originally published: c1982
Summary: Simple text and scenes depict times when it is good to
have self control, such as listening when you want to talk, waiting,
sacrificing the biggest piece of candy, and being a good loser.
ISBN 1-56766-306-0 (hardcover)
1. Self-control in children—Juvenile literature.   [1. Self-control.]
I. Title.
BF723.S25G36   1996
179'.9—dc20   96-11864
                              CIP
                              AC

The Child's World of
SELF-CONTROL

By Henrietta Gambill • Illustrated by Mechelle Ann

THE CHILD'S WORLD

What is self-control?

Self-control is listening to your friend talk when you want him to listen to you!

Letting someone else take the biggest piece of candy takes self-control. And waiting until after dinner to eat your piece takes even more!

Letting your cat down to play when she wiggles takes self-control, because it's such fun to hold her close and listen to her purr.

Not laughing when your sister falls down—that takes a LOT of self-control.

When your baby sister is asleep and you want to play with her—but instead you tiptoe quietly out—that's having self-control.

And self-control is not feeding the dog when he begs at the table.

When your team loses because you struck out, self-control keeps you from throwing your bat on the ground.

Being quiet in the library takes self-control, especially when a friend comes in and you want to call to her.

Self-control is lining up when the teacher asks you to—and not pushing the person in front of you!

Self-control is waiting for the scissors—without complaining—when you and a friend are sharing a pair.

And when you don't know the answers, self-control is keeping your eyes on your own paper.

Self-control means you really think and decide what is right for you to do.

Can you think of other ways to show self-control?